Fey Lights

LIANA BROOKS

OTHER WORKS

ALL I WANT FOR CHRISTMAS
All I Want For Christmas Is A Werewolf
All I Want For Christmas Is A Reaper

FLEET OF MALIK
Bodies In Motion
Change of Momentum

HEROES AND VILLAINS
Even Villains Fall In Love
Even Villains Go To The Movies
Even Villains Have Interns
Even Villains Play The Hero (omnibus)
The Polar Terror

TIME AND SHADOWS MYSTERIES
The Day Before
Convergence Point
Decoherence

SHORTER WORKS
Darkness and Good
Fey Lights
Prime Sensations

Find other works by the author at www.lianabrooks.com.

Fey Lights

LIANA BROOKS

AUSTRALIA

Print ISBN-13: 978-1-925825-96-1
eBook ISBN: 9781502238306

www.inkprintpress.com

National Library of Australia Cataloguing-in-Publication Data
Brooks, Liana 1982 –
Fey Lights
72 p.   cm.
ISBN-13: 978-1-925825-96-1
Inkprint Press, Canberra, Australia
1. Fiction—Romance—Science Fiction 2. Fiction—Science Fiction—Space Opera

First Print Edition: February 2015
Second Edition: November 2020

Cover design © Inkprint Press

DEDICATION

This is for Laurie and the rest of the SFR Brigade crew who gave my crazy imagination a safe port to land in. Here's to always finding your true home.

For the Tweeps who inspire my insanity, especially Bill.
For my friends who get me through my rough days.
For my betas who are awesome beyond description.
For my children, who always make me laugh.

And for my husband—after ten years together you're still my hero. I love you.

FEY LIGHTS

Dark water writhed over the ship's deck, a living thing hunting for prey, stinging like acid where it touched bare skin. Jeani stumbled over the guts of her ship, swearing in every language she knew. Her foot fell through a hole in the deck created by the crash. Hot metal gouged her leg as tears ran down her cheeks.

I don't want to die like this. There has to be a way out.

There is *a way out. The same way the water is coming in.*

Running was out of the question. Half-limping, half-swimming through the rising water, Jeani forced herself back to the rear of the ship, navigating by touch and the weak glow of the emergency lights that hadn't burst, back to the gaping wound that was once the engine room and secondary hold. Pressure from the rapid descent into the gravity well and the gushing water warped the frame, creating a strong current. Jeani grabbed the free-fall handle near the emergency door and pressed her free hand to the glowing lock.

Nothing.

She tried yanking the override.

Nothing.

She kicked the door with her good leg.

Pressure sent the door flying inwards at the head of a tidal wave. Jeani gasped for air and went under. Seconds ticked away as she grappled blindly for the next free-fall handle, the current tugging at her.

The hand-hold slipped out of her grip. She pushed up once, bumping her head against the high ceiling of the engine room as she gasped for air. The current swirled under her, pulling her down into the darkness. Saltwater stung her face. She shuddered as something nipped at her bleeding leg. Ignoring the pain, she clawed at the water until she broke through and gasped in the alien atmosphere. Water crashed over her in the darkness.

Rough, warm sand rubbed against her skin. Sucking in a lungful of the oxygen-rich air, Jeani flipped onto her stomach and pulled herself away from the water. It lapped at her legs, a wayward lover begging her to return.

She laughed as she looked at the strange stars overhead. Her lungs burned, her leg ached, she was shaking with delayed shock, but she was alive. "See, Hothi, I told you I wasn't going to die that easy."

Dominique pushed through the crowd and looked down at the beach.

"Could be a Lander," Gregor said as he adjusted his cap. "Saw the prison ships sailing past this last moon. Could be a Lander," he repeated with a final snort.

A knife waved past Dominique's face, stabbing toward the figure on the beach. "'Twere wedding lights last night. Lit up the sky with fire, set the trees to burning," said Beau.

"'Tain't no fire touched the trees. Trees are fine," Gregor argued. "'Tis a Lander."

"Fey fire," someone said behind him. "Fey burn things with cold fire." A fist hit Dominique's shoulder. "Fey can turn a man's bones to ice. They summon monsters from the deep."

One of the women crossed her fingers and made the sign of the arch to ward off the ill will of the deep dwellers.

"Landers bring plague," Adrian said grimly. He too tapped Dominique's shoulder. "We can't let a Lander near the village."

"We's best shooting it from here," Gregor said.

Another shook his head. "Arrows can't touch fey."

"You volunteering to go down there to slit its throat?" Gregor demanded.

"Such a thing to ask a man! I've got kin, I have."

There was the sound of shuffling feet. A cool sea breeze wrapped around Dominique's legs as the crowd parted. He filled their silence with imagined conversations. "He's a Lander," one would say in the Silent way of the island-born. "Got no kin nor woman of his own, does he," someone else would murmur. Dominique kept the snarl he felt forming in his throat from escaping.

"Will you go?" Adrian whispered, confirming his suspicions. "None will make you, if you say no."

"You'll go?" Dominique asked with a half-smile. Adrian wasn't a bad man. Island born, birthed in the sea, born running on the beach and listening to the waves. The island-born claimed the waves spoke back to those that listened. The saltwater seeped into their blood so they could hear the thoughts of others like they heard the song of the ocean. Like all the island born, Adrian had no trouble believing every infamy laid against the Landers who lived on the far side of the ocean, in the land of the tyrant.

Adrian shrugged. "Better to slit the Lander's throat on the beach than let it breathe on a child in the village. We'll all die of black blood and fever before the tide is high."

"I'll go," Dominique said, loud enough for his voice to carry to the back of the crowd. "I'll go see to the Lander. I'll send him down to the docks in the south. He can find work there if he likes."

"What if it be fey?" Gregor asked, eyes wide.

Dominique studied the lone figure on the distant sand below, a sad creature sprawled under the hot morning sun. "The fey have a treaty with the Tyrant of Urull. The first tyrant traded his soul for the secrets of the fey lights—wedding lights," he corrected himself, using the island-born term. "The first tyrant lost his mind when the fey showed him the wonders of their world. Men that could turn into dogs. Deep monsters that could walk as men. Women so beautiful that they could suck the soul of a man as he walked past, steal his life with a kiss.

"The tyrants all have made a pact with the fey, traded their subjects to the fey for their favor, but they've never let the fey roam the lands. No fey walk outside the tyrant's gates in Urull. No fey step on the white sands of the islands."

"Maybe this one is outcast," Beau said. "A prisoner, like all the other Landers sent here."

"You've got a leak in your hull," Adrian said, punching Beau in the arm. "You think the tyrant could make a prisoner out of the fey? You think a man could keep one of them under lock and key?"

"But... wedding lights!" Beau looked to Dominique for support. "The lights haven't touched our sky in years."

"No one's been out walking in years," Dominique said. "Who was out last night?" He turned and scanned the crowd. Hardy folk, the island-born. They wore homespun cloth, britches of old sail cloth traded from down the coast, filigree gold necklaces twined around shells and sea gems. All of them came from Lander families at some point in their history, Landers who had either escaped the tyrants, or been banished to a slow death on the distant islands, depending on who you asked. But the islands were in their blood now. They spoke in Silence, and left him an outcast. The women looked away from him, the older men met his gaze, and one boy blushed. "Tris? Were you out walking last night?"

The boy with dark eyes and a thatch of red hair looked up. "May have been. What's it to you?"

Someone chuckled.

"Explains the wedding lights," Gregor muttered. "You still ought to slit the throat first. That one's not going to give you any answer you'll be wanting."

DOMINIQUE LEANED AGAINST A TREE AND PONDERED THE strange scene before him. Something had melted the sand near the mouth of the bay. A stain of blood colored the beach not far from the glass. Fey or Lander, the body was gone. He pushed away from the tree, slid his knife into its sheath, and walked the length of the beach.

Lightning sometimes struck the sand and left strange spirals buried there, but this was different. He squatted down and broke a piece of brittle glass off the sand. No natural force he'd ever heard of made plates of glass with bubbles and debris, as if someone had dragged fire across the beach. He glanced at the clear blue sky, half expecting to see multicolored fire raining down. Wedding lights, fey lights, plague lights, call them what you would, he'd never known them to bring anything good.

Standing up, he brushed sand from his britches. Something cold wrapped around his wrist and twisted his arm up against his back. Cool steel kissed his throat.

"Tell me those three little words I need to hear," a woman's voice purred near his ear in the heavily accented Tradespeak that Landers favored. Dominique tried stepping back, but she compensated and twisted his arm harder. "Tell me."

What three little words did a woman need to hear? "I love you?"

"I love you?" There was a curl of confusion and laughter in her words. A face peeked around his shoulder. Hair black as the abyss, knotted by waves and littered with seaweed. Eyes teal and bright like the bay waters, and skin a deep, dark tan that wasn't native to any Lander or island-born that he had ever seen. She raised her eyebrow. "You love me? Don't you think it's a little early for that?"

"What did you want me to say?" he asked.

"I am human?" she suggested, nodding.

He smiled. "I am human." She let go of his wrist and stepped back out of reach. "Is that something you need to worry after?" Dominique drank in the sight of her. Black cloth britches hung loose from her slim waist. A much tighter black shirt with long sleeves now ripped by the tide revealed pale marks in an ivy leaf pattern... His heart hammered in his chest.

No Lander alive would wear black so casually, the color the plague victims wore to warn others. The color his sister had worn when he saw her the last time, watching from the dockside in Urull. The color the woman he loved wore the first time they'd met, a ragged black dress and a tattoo of ivy leaves running down her arm.

"When one finds oneself in the middle of nowhere it's best to clarify what species one is dealing with." Her serious mien changed to an impish smile. "It could happen." She didn't bother to clarify what "it" was, just stuck her hands on her hips and regarded the surf with distaste.

"You're on the islands," Dominique said, stepping closer. His heart drummed louder than the surf. He had to know if it was her, if she remembered him, if she still loved him...

He wanted to touch her skin, see if it was as warm as he remembered. Her lips would taste of salt, like the sea, like they had the first time they kissed...

She was exactly the kind of woman who could tease men into the watery depths to drown.

"'Island' is really not a descriptive term," she said without seeming to realize he was approaching.

"There are only a handful of islands. What more do you want to know?" Dominique reached for her hair.

She dodged, stumbling as her leg buckled under her. Snarling, she staggered back like a wounded animal. "Don't touch me."

Dominique held up his hands in surrender.

"Tell me where we are. I need to get out of here before Hothi finds me."

"Hothi?"

Her eyes grew cold. "You know Hothi?"

He shook his head.

"Do you know where he took Ulric?"

"I've never heard of Hothi before in my life."

"You're one of them. I can smell the Finn blood running in your veins. It doesn't matter if you're with him or not, Hothi's gone rogue, and I'll see him burn. Morgan wouldn't believe me, but I'll see him burn." She shivered, and rubbed her arm. Blood seeped through her shirt where she touched it.

Dominique caught her as she swayed. Her blood was red as his, but she was no island-born or Lander. He'd known it the first time he'd seen her lying on the streets of Urull, the first time he'd carried her home and cared for her as she healed. It seemed he was bound to do it again.

He carried her through the jungle to the wood hut he called home. It wasn't as grand as the tall buildings of Urull—no paintings or bedrooms with colored walls—but it was his, built by hand to suit his needs.

He'd never brought a woman back here because the only woman he'd wanted all these years—the one he'd searched relentlessly for as he traveled from Urull to the isles to the far sea—was the one he carefully laid on his bed now.

The tattoo was gone, vibrant green ink replaced by pale scars. Her hair was no longer the short, raggedy mess he remembered. She looked healthier now. Her skin didn't cling to bone. There were muscles now, and curves.

He found himself tracing the familiar curve of her lips, and stopped himself. There would be time for touching later. Now she needed to rest and heal.

JEANI WOKE TO THE SHARP SMELL OF OCEAN SALT. FOR A moment she thought she was stuck in that hideous cave on the Plains of Abrinth with Morgan again. A breeze perfumed by alien flowers brushed past her. The Plains of Abrinth had no breeze, although there had been a mighty strong current. The fever that had claimed her in the first hours as her body adjusted to the alien bacteria had subsided, leaving her achy. It took a moment to force herself to stand up.

Stretching as she walked, she wandered the room, looking at the trinkets the stranger kept, brushing her fingers over a polished chair. She explored the small kitchen area with a rough block of smoothed wood for a counter and a small metal stove for cooking, but empty of any food she recognized. All the cloth was undyed, but everything else she saw was a vibrant shade of blue or purple. Countless rocks were strewn around the one-room house, all of them shiny, all of them large. Jeani gently nudged one with her bare foot. When nothing happened she moved on.

The Finn's smell was everywhere, a combination of sun, sea and man rubbed into every surface. It was a smell both familiar and forbidding. A long-buried memory fought for her attention, but she shoved it ruthlessly away. That was from her life before, the life of Old Jeani. The memory could taunt her forever, but she wasn't the sort of woman to run off on a whim any more. She had responsibilities now, and she wasn't the only one who died if she failed.

Behind a sheet of thick cloth, she found rough shelves with folded linen. She took refuge there and changed out of her ripped biosuit, checking for injuries as she did. Her arms had healed well, but the gash on her leg was still red and raw.

"Your tattoos are gone," said a deep voice.

She spun around, rubbing her scarred arm out of habit. On the other side of the sheet the Finn dropped something wooden on the floor. "What do you know about that?" The photosynthetic tattoos with their addictive buzz were long gone. She'd had the last of the bacteria burned out after her first battle with withdrawal.

Only a few sharp-eyed friends knew that the drugs had ever been part of her life.

"They were distinctive," he said from the other side of the sheet. The bed creaked under his weight as he sat on it. "I thought they were beautiful."

"They were killing me." Grabbing blindly, she pulled an undyed shirt over her head. It felt strange against her skin, rough, scratchy, but it would have to do until she could find the port. "I don't do that sort of thing anymore. I'm an enforcer now." She pulled the sheet back with what she hoped was her best imperious glare. "And I'm on a mission."

The man on the bed smiled at her sadly, navy blue eyes dark with an emotion she couldn't name.

Jeani straightened her shoulders. Standing barefoot in front of a man who towered over her while wearing a shirt five sizes too large didn't give her a commanding presence. Endless Night, but she would kill for six more inches of height on days like this. She raised an eyebrow as his gaze roamed over her. "Gotten your eyeful? Can we go now?"

He stood up. "You don't remember me, do you?"

"The only Finn I know is Morgan. He doesn't discuss family with me." Although she'd love to hear that Morgan talked about her to his kin. Morgan was the Finn equivalent of an enforcer in this sector. They'd butted heads over cases on a regular basis.

"I don't know Morgan, but I know you. Topaz."

She froze. Memories long locked away tumbled over her. Memories of a dying city shrouded in a dark smog, of a thin woman whose knuckles bled from her work, of a boy not quite a man who whispered he loved her as she fought the terrors and depression of withdrawal... "Min?"

He moved closer, eyes bright with joy. "You do remember."

"Is Petra here?"

Min's steps faltered. "She was taken by black blood fever not long after you left. She knew she was sick early on, long enough for her to buy passage for me to the islands." He turned away, walking to the sunlit door. "I thought I would find you here, if I searched enough. I'd given up, and now I find you half dead on the beach. Why is it that every time I find you, you're half-dead?"

Jeani shrugged apologetically. "I couldn't be witty or pretty so I settled for a talent that was within my scope. I'm really good at getting beaten up and gasping for air."

Min returned to her. "I remember other talents." He kissed her forehead.

She closed her eyes, basking in the warmth of his touch for a moment. "I can't stay."

Min shrunk back in confusion, shoulders hunching as he frowned. "You just came back to me."

"I wish I could stay." She reached for him without thinking, and then stopped herself. "I need to go, to protect you, to find Ulric, to stop a plague. I'm sorry. Staying here is just asking for trouble. Take me to the port. Please?"

"Dominique!" A man's voice echoed outside in the fading evening light. "Are you here?"

Dominique. She'd never known his full name. Petra had always called him Min, and Jeani had never asked for any other name.

"It's Adrian," he said. "I was supposed to slit your throat and send you back to sea before you could bring the plague here."

"Then you should stop holding me and go talk to your friend." She watched him go. Again. With a leaden feeling she sat on the bed. The days in Urull had been bad. Without sunlight to power her tat, the byproduct of her symbiotic bacteria had died. Her buzz was gone.

In retrospect she was able to admit that Petra had saved her, rescued her from the whorehouse, and dragged her out of the drugged haze.

The memories of that year were vague. She could still feel the warmth of the drug coursing in her veins, and hear Petra's stern voice. And then... Min.

His voice haunted her dreams as he sang her lullabies in a foreign language, held her hand, kissed her... She shook her head. Of all the times to run into him again. If this were a routine mission, if she just had to worry about reporting back in, if Ulric's life wasn't on the line... So many ifs.

She lay in the bed, drifting in and out of healing sleep until the morning birds began to sing. Angry voices woke her. She grabbed her soggy boots from a puddle of seawater and shoved her feet into them.

Outside, a dozen other men of varying sizes sat around a large fire. The morning sun was peeking over the horizon, but they all had the look of men who had spent the dark hours talking too long. Dominique stood when she stepped outside, his eyes dark and wide in the half-light.

"Good morning," she said in Standard.

There was a shuffling among the men, and the smell of fear almost overran the smell of Sanguis, un-mutated humans.

Dominique walked toward her with a shy smile. "Good morning." His Standard had a stronger accent now.

The other men started talking all at once in the native dialect. None of the words they said were familiar, but Jeani understood the body language. They were scared. They were angry. They didn't want her here. She touched Min's arm. "Tell them I'm leaving."

He frowned in disagreement.

"Tell them I want to go away. I don't plan to stay here. If you will tell me where the port is, I'll go. Just point me in the right direction."

Not breaking eye contact, he said something to the others in the native language. They still smelled of fear.

"I won't hurt anyone," she promised.

Dominique watched her, eyes smiling. "They don't like you in a man's shirt, even if it is mine."

Jeani glanced down the rough shirt that flapped loosely, several sizes too large. "Should I change?"

He nodded solemnly.

Shrugging, she reached for the hem of the shirt and began pulling it off. Strong hands grabbed her arms.

"Not here," Dominique whispered in her ear. He was so close she could hear his racing heartbeat.

"You said they wanted me to change. If wearing another person's shirt is that offensive I can go naked until I find the port."

He tugged her shirt down across her belly. "You can't walk around without clothes."

"Why not? How can skin be offensive?"

His dark blue eyes searched her face, trying to find what she couldn't guess. "Wear my shirt. Eat my food. It will be well."

She shrugged again. "If you insist." Jeani let the shirt drop.

The other men hurried away, casting curious glances over their shoulders as they left.

"They think you're fey. You scare them," Dominique said. "Do you want food?"

There was a large black pot hanging over the open fire that smelled of dead things and ocean. It was probably fish. She wrinkled her nose. "I'd rather get going. I need to get to the port before Hothi finds me."

Dominique stepped away from her, brow knitted in frustration. He walked to the fire and removed the pot in silence.

"Which name do you prefer, Min or Dominique?" Jeani asked.

Crossing his arms, he studied her for a quiet moment before answering, "They call me Dominique Thierry. You're still Topaz? Or is there a better name for you?"

"I'm Jeani D'Bellfrie Tigya of Nile. Yes, it's the famous artist's colony. No, I can't paint anything." She laughed. "Two decades after our first kiss and we're finally properly introduced." With a sigh, she looked around the idyllic little jungle glen that Dominique had made his home. "I need to get to the port before Hothi does. The sooner we leave, the better."

"The port isn't going to run away because you don't get there by midday."

"You've never met Hothi."

Dominique cocked his head to the side. "What did this Hothi do to you?"

"It's not what he did to me. It's what I did to him, and what he's going to do for revenge. That's his ship at the bottom of the bay." Jeani took a deep breath and caught the scent of fresh bread under the odors of dead fish and smelly Finn. "Where's the bread?"

"By the water bucket," Dominique pointed to something behind her.

She looked around, and saw a crude water barrel sitting under the corner of the house with a wrapped loaf of bread beside it. "Thank you." Flipping back the cloth covering the bread, she frowned. "Is it supposed to be green?"

"The women in the village gather seaweed to make the flour."

Jeani grimaced. "Does it taste worse than lizard?"

"I've never had lizard. Is that what they eat in the fey realms?"

"It's what you eat when you're in enforcer training and can't find anything else. If you ever want to lose obscene amounts of weight, take survival training with a Rus. They don't understand that normal people need food at regular intervals." She broke off a chunk of the green bread and tried a bite. It tasted of licorice. Not something you'd spread berry jam on, but it didn't make her gag outright. "I liked Petra's recipe better. Can we leave for port?" she asked between mouthfuls.

"Let me get my trade pack. I'll walk with you and see if I can't make it worth my while to go."

D OMINIQUE WIPED A BEAD OF SWEAT FROM HIS FACE, cursing himself for taking the jungle paths instead of following the shoreline where the heat wasn't so oppressive. As he took a swig of water from his canteen, he turned to look for Jeani. He'd set a brutal pace to mollify her impatience, but every so often she seemed to forget her desire to reach port and wandered off.

This time she'd stopped to inspect a glowing lily. A spotted leopard moth fluttered down from the high canopy and landed on the lily. Diaphanous white petals enfolded the moth as the flower devoured its prey.

Jeani quirked an eyebrow up, then spun around to face him. "When will we reach the port?"

"Before midday." Dominique resettled the travel pack on his shoulder.

Wood carvings sold well when the prison ships were in port. With luck, they'd arrive while the Landers were still sleeping off their trip, but before the crew left port. If the ship hadn't sailed on the morning tide, there was a good chance to turn a profit. A little rice flour, or a few yards of woven cloth, something to persuade Jeani to stay with him.

A cold wind whipped through the trees. Dominique looked around as the hot air resettled around them.

"Problems?" Jeani asked, catching up to him without complaint.

"Possibly. We'll be able to tell once we make it to the ridge." Picking up the pace, he led her to fey ridge that divided the two halves of the island. From there he'd be able to see the ocean, and the sky. Cold winds on a hot day did not bode well.

He reached the ridge with Jeani at his heels and stared at the horizon.

"A storm?" Jeani asked without the fearful tone of the island-born. Sons of the tyrant, any Lander whose brain wasn't pickled by the sleeping juice used to quell prison riots would know to fear a storm.

"Maybe..." He watched the clouds, waiting to see how they moved. One of the huge gray puffs in the distance seemed a little too fast. A trick of the wind?

"We never had good storms in Euphrate. Up on the mesa all the clouds go beneath us. The rain fills the wells, but rain at that altitude is rare. I remember the first time it rained, everyone pulled out their canvases and the entire mesa was covered in a cloth rainbow—"

The gray storm cloud picked up speed. "

Run!" Dominique ordered, grabbing her arm. "Run for the trees! It's not a storm!" Dominique shouted, but his words were swallowed as the chill gale ripped across the mountainside.

He checked the beast again. Silver tentacles unfurled from the cloud, lightning crackling between them as the creature rushed toward the island. Dropping his pack near the path, Dominique ran after the fey woman. A stranger to the islands, she couldn't possibly understand what was coming.

The sudden change in temperature turned the humid air into a cold fog with clinging rain. His foot slipped as the dust of the mountain path became slick mud.

A cry of dismay came from ahead.

Dominique pushed to his feet and ran faster. Jeani had stopped at the bend in the ridge road, looking down at the obscured port with an expression of horror. Dominique studied the scene. Port La Hache and the placid waters of Barataria Bay sat below them, unaware of the storm approaching the high reaches. Already the fog was creeping through the jungle forest with icy tentacles.

"Where are the ships?" Jeani asked. "Where is everyone?"

Dominique looked at the two, tall-masted prison ships and the small flotilla of fishing vessels. "Right there. We need to go." He tugged at her arm, trying to pull her to the safety of the trees.

"Those are boats!" Her voice hit a panicked octave. "You said this was a port, not a boathouse."

"It's a port for sailing vessels," he said slowly.

"And I want a spaceport for spaceships!" She turned to him, eyes wide in manic expression.

A tree cracked in the forest, dying under the fiery touch of the beast. "We need to find cover before the beast reaches us." The rising fog thickened, hiding the ridge, the path, and the jungle from his sight. "Please. I'll give you a home."

"What beast?" Jeani asked as her grip tightened.

"A deep beast. They pull people from the ground to eat them. Please, come. If we stay here we'll be caught," he answered as the fog enveloped them.

"Where do we hide?"

He took her hand and shuffled forward, walking along the ridge from memory. Jeani said nothing. Lost in the fog where shattered sunlight became pieces of rainbow, he could hear her quiet breathing, and for a brief moment the world was deceptively calm.

Blue light crackled to their right as a tentacle fell from the clouds only a few man-lengths away. Dominique pulled Jeani to him and moved to the left of the path. A tentacle dropped in front of them, close enough for him to feel the heat on his face.

"What's Plan B?" Jeani asked in a whisper that tickled his ear.

"The monster can't hear us," Dominique said, even though he wasn't sure if that was true. He sucked in a breath. "We could run."

"We could split up," Jeani suggested. She titled her face skywards. "Or hit it. How do you kill something that size?"

"Feed it to a very larger snapper," he said. Another tentacle stabbed behind them. "The longer we stand still..."

"Yes. Run!" Jeani sprinted away into the fog.

Three steps, and she was lost to his sight. The air around him crackled and the blue lightning of the tentacle surrounded him.

JEANI SKIDDED INTO A TREE. BOUNCING HER FACE OFF A TREE was just the sort of thing Morgan would tease her about, if she somehow managed to get off this Finn-cursed planet. If Morgan was still alive. If she didn't get bumped back to first level enforcer.

Ancestors in the Endless Night, if this mission went any worse the directorate would probably hand her a paintbrush and send her back to Euphrate. She'd crashed a stolen vessel, possibly spread new diseases to the natives, and now had close contact with—

A man's scream split the fog.

"Dominique?" Curse her hide. She'd lost him in the fog assuming he could take care of himself. *Stupid, Jeani, stupid.*

None of her classes had covered a xenopredator like this. Probably because the class was taught by a Rus and flying jellyfish couldn't possibly be edible. Probably. It was so hard to tell with the Rus.

Think, girl. Tentacles like an electric eel. So, what did you do that time on the Plains of Abrinth? Disconnect and sever.

Jeani searched for a dead tree branch. Dominique screamed again as she snatched one up and ran toward the monster. She found Dominique on hands and knees, shaking and vomiting violently.

A tentacle lashed down. She struck, swinging the branch and catching the tentacle. Straining with all her might, she brought the tentacle down to the dirt at Dominique's side. The monster wailed, a high-pitched, shrill note like wind tearing across the mesa, as blue light arched and danced into the dirt path. Puddles of water shimmered with strange light. Her hair frizzed as the electricity discharged through the ground.

The noise ceased and the tentacle went limp.

Jeani laughed in surprise. "I didn't think that would work." She looked up, and only had a moment to assess the situation before she threw herself at Dominique and pushed him back as the dead beast collapsed on them. It was like being buried under a giant wet blanket. Kicking created a small pocket, but didn't free them.

Dominique rolled to his side. His arm flopped over her shoulder as he coughed and shivered, twitching at odd intervals. She stroked his hair back until his eyes focused.

Nervously, she giggled. "I think we grounded it."

He rubbed his face as he blinked. "Grounded it?" His voice was raw.

She kicked at the monstrosity again. This time her foot went through the barrier and came away oozing.

"It probably used helium to float, or maybe hydrogen gas. Do you think the electric sting was a means of defense, prey capture, or a by-product of the conversion process?"

Dominique coughed. "I think I understood a few of the small words."

Her cheeks turned warm. "Sorry, I babble like that when I'm nervous. It is a very interesting animal though. Are they common here?" Gray goo dripped between them and steamed. "This will be a fun story to tell when I get home." She snorted. "Another fine mess. Crash the ship. Get lost, and then get stuck under a flying jellyfish. Morgan is never going to let me live this one down."

"Mmm." Dominique's eyes closed.

Jeani wiggled an arm free and touched his face. "Are you all right?"

"Mmm-hmm." One eye popped open. "Your voice is restful."

"Right. I suppose a little shock therapy is bound to make even a Finn tired. I'll poke you if something interesting happens."

By her count it took an hour for the creature to dis-solve into little more than lumps of undigested aquatic victims and a small beak-like ring of hard material, which could have been its mouth or the remains of a squid. She couldn't tell. Leaving Dominique on the ground snoring, she walked to the ledge overlooking his port. Nothing but boats. There were wooly animals with packs, but no motorized ground transport. The boats had cloth sails, not the solar powered steamer cells she'd seen on other rural planets. The chances of finding a spaceship down there, even a small one, were astronomically low.

She glanced back at Dominique. If he was telling the truth, the only spaceport she could remember was across the ocean on the wrong side of the planet, and it was entirely possible she'd taken the last spaceship out.

"Ancestors!" She kicked a rock over the ledge in frustration. Her ship was Finn biotech. Borrowed Finn biotech. She had a better chance of Morgan showing up and demanding to know where his old runabout was than she did of the ship repairing itself any time in the next century.

Maybe, if all the lucky stars in the universe aligned in her favor, the ship might repair itself quickly. Unfortunately, she was almost positive the nano-core had ruptured during the crash, and without it the hull was nothing more than a future reef habitat.

She hit the palm of her hand on her forehead. The directorate didn't have protocol for situations like this. *Keis.* Maybe this is what had happened to Ulric; he hadn't been captured, he'd been stranded. Hothi knew where Ulric was, she was certain of that. The connections were too strong to ignore.

Gravel skittered in the path beside her. "What are you thinking that makes you frown?" Dominique asked as he sat beside her.

"I'm wondering if Ulric is here or if someone will come looking for me."

"Ulric?" Dominique frowned. "I thought your lover was Morgan."

She raised an eyebrow. "Excuse me?"

"You said Morgan's name several times. I thought you and he were wed."

"No. Morgan Finn is the..." She scrambled for the proper term. "The designate, I think, for this region. He's in charge of watching what little travel comes this way and keeping things regulated as the Patriarch sees fit. Ulric is a whole other problem entirely."

Dominique nodded slowly. "Is Ulric your lover?"

"Enforcer Ulric de Leon is a pain in my side, the missing grandson to the Empress De Leon of Savannah, and... Wait, you haven't seen a seven foot tall, golden-colored man, have you? Tan skin, gold or blue eyes, dark gold hair? He might change into a lion occasionally, or eat things. Weird things."

"A lion?" Dominique was frowning again.

"He's an exomorph de Leon." She shook her head when he didn't answer. "Do you know what a lion is?" He shook his head. "An exomorph?" Another shake. "Have you ever heard of the Felinium?"

"I only know of the Tyrants in Urull. If the other islands have empresses and beasts made of gold, I've never heard. I don't travel that far and I can't speak the Silence of the island-born."

She tried to run her fingers through her hair, but

they tangled in the gray ooze. "How about shower? Is that a word you know?"

DOMINIQUE OFFERED JEANI A CLOTH TOWEL, WHICH SHE took with a heavy sigh as she glared at his washing area. He didn't see the problem. It was the same as all the baths in the island-born villages, a copper bowl with a small door that could be opened to let the sun-warmed water fall on the body. It was more than he had ever had living on the streets of Urull, but Jeani seemed to think baths should be indoors, and heated. She glowered as she snapped the privacy screen shut and muttered in a strange, lyrical language.

Dominique sat there, letting the sun bake off the crusted slime and easing his sore muscles, as he mused over her words. Ships from space? What kind of space would ships move in?

His heart ached. She truly was not from this world. Her exotic beauty wasn't a twist of fate, it was a true sign of her strangeness, but she was trapped here. There was no husband waiting for her on the other side of the fey lights.

If she was trapped here in his world, could he convince her to stay on the islands? Could he please her? Win her for himself?

She stepped out of the bath and his heart wasn't the only thing that stirred. The drying cloth he'd given her barely covered enough for decency. Long legs stole his breath.

She walked on tiptoe across the ground, jumping from rock to rock to keep off the dirt. Every step seemed designed to rivet his gaze on her softest curves. Just before she reached him, she stilled. A soft pink blush touched her cheeks.

"Sorry," she said, tucking a strand of wet hair behind her ear. "I wasn't sure if the no nudity rule applied when your friends weren't around, but this is ridiculously short. Can I have clothes now, or drop this? Either one works for me."

Dominique stood up, drawn to her. He stopped inches away from the fey temptress. "May I kiss you?"

Jeani's eyebrows went up. "Don't you want a shower first?"

"No." Dominique's lips brushed over hers. Her breath caught and she leaned into him, mouth opening, inviting him in with the flick of her tongue. She tasted of honey and sunshine. He groaned as he reached for her, pulling her closer.

She laughed, pushing him away. "You really do need a shower."

A siren, that's what she was. Teal eyes sparkled, tempting him to taste delights beyond the ken of men. "After the shower?"

"After... Maybe."

He leaned forward to steal another quick kiss. "One of the village folk brought clothes up while we were away. There's a skirt and such, if you like them."

A quick, cold shower in fresh water and then he dressed in the bathing stall. Cold water had done nothing to kill his appetite. Jeani was waiting for him, sitting in the sunlight in a simple skirt and blouse that only highlighted every delight of her luscious body.

She smiled. "Do prisoners get lunch around here?"

That brought him up short. "Prisoner?"

"Refugee?" she asked. "Exile? What would you call me?"

Dominique walked past her into the house, his plans for a lazy, naked afternoon derailed. "Where are you from?"

"I told you, Euphrate on Nile."

"That means nothing to me."

"How could it mean nothing to you? Your people reduced our planet to a desert! You stole our oceans. That doesn't ring any bells?"

Dominique stared at her. "The Tyrant did that?"

"The Finn did that. Your people, not the natives to this planet."

He sliced salted meat and layered on a white spread she hoped was a cheese. "I was born in Urull, under the shadow of the Tyrant."

"Born here, maybe, but you aren't a native," Jeani said as she took the offered sandwich. "You don't fit in, do you? You're bigger than the locals, taller, more muscular? You age slower, heal faster, move quicker. If there's a brawl you'll win every time."

His eye twitched at the description. "How did you know that?"

"I know Finns. They're like my kind, genetically engineered humans. Finns were the first," she said in a singsong voice of someone reciting a poem from memory. "First to find their second skin, first to walk the stars. Second came the de Leon, matriarch to the patriarch, Empress of the Pride. Third were the Rus, the white tigers and lone hunters. Fourth came the Tigya, perfection of form and function. Fifth came the Pantros, the stealthy, cunning ones. Never trust a Pantros." She took a bite of her sandwich. "I'm a Tigya. The poem's a little biased, and it leaves off some of the lesser races, but it was written by a Tigya so I suppose that explains it."

He finished his lunch and poured them both water. "What is a 'second skin'?"

"Thank you," Jeani said as she took the offered water. "A second skin is the main mutation. Finns, de Leon, Rus, Tigya, Pantros... all of them are shapeshifters. Well." She hiccupped and blushed. "Not all. All the exomorphs are shapeshifters. Mesomorphs have half forms, usually whiskers or a tail on an other-wise human body. I'm an endomorph. I can't change forms. At home, it's a problem, but it's a useful skill for an enforcer who gets stuck on Sanguis planets too often. No one can force me to change shape as proof that I'm an alien."

Dominique stood up and paced. "You really aren't from one of the islands?"

"No."

"You're from fairy land?"

"No, I'm from a planet, those big rocks in the sky that fly around stars."

"All I've ever seen are stars."

Jeani shrugged. "I didn't say the planets were close. They exist though. There isn't magic, just science. A little genetic tinkering and a man becomes something more. It's straightforward enough, just don't ask me about the technical bits. My job is enforcing Felinium law, not rearranging molecules." She chuckled weakly. "My job was, I guess. Now I'm something of a professional island castaway."

He tried to match her smile as he processed what she had told him. Worlds full of people like him. More than just island-born or Landers. Whole other worlds, not just islands. Even in his wildest dreams he'd never imagined something so spectacular. Maybe there was even a place where men turned into dogs. "The sun is setting. Come outside and tell me which star is yours."

They lay together in the hammock, looking at the stars. Jeani would point to one and tell him the name, and about the people who lived there. All the diverse cultures and strange sights she'd seen in her hunt for the missing Ulric that had led her into battle against the slaver, Hothi. He held her close.

"Could you be happy here? Without all of your wonders and marvels?"

She wiggled closer, one leg casually laid over his. "It won't be forever. My ship will repair itself one day, or someone will come looking for me. Morgan knows I'm here. Hothi will come eventually, to make sure I'm dead if nothing else. I can be patient until they come. What's a handful of decades after all?"

"I don't know if I can be so careless about so many years."

"How old are you?" Jeani asked.

"I don't know. Years are a strange thing to count when you're wandering the islands. I know I first left Urull when Adrian was small. I met him as a small boy trading at the docks with his father. I only settled here after Adrian's wedding two years ago."

She gave him a funny look. "You can't keep track of years, but you can keep track of one boy's life?" Her head rested on his chest as her eyes drifted closed.

"People are easier to remember than days."

Bright blue-green lights rocketed across the sky. "Look!" Dominique pointed. "Wedding lights! The island-born say that if you see wedding lights with a person you've found your true love."

Jeani twisted to look up, and jumped out of the hammock. "Ships!" She waved her arms. "Those are ships! Where are they going?"

One wedding light became two, then four, then seven. "They're going to Urull, to see the Tyrant."

"How far away is Urull?"

"Too far to swim. Too far for any of the village ships to travel. The water runs deep, and there are monsters there. The only ships that brave the passage are the prison ships bringing new Landers to the islands. But even the Tyrant's fastest ship takes over a day to reach the port of Urull." He took her hand. "Is that your Morgan looking for you?"

"No, it's probably Hothi coming to steal slaves and put a bounty on my head. *Keis*! Hothi knows where Ulric is, I'm sure of it. Ulric was hunting him when he vanished. I wouldn't put it past him to have Ulric wrapped up in chains on his ship. And I'm stuck on the wrong side of the planet!"

Dominique pulled her back to the hammock. "Tomorrow I'll see if I can find a large fishing vessel. Maybe we can find our way there. For tonight, stay with me?"

Jeani hesitated, then fell back into the hammock beside him. "Wedding lights? Is that really what you call them?"

"It's what the island-born call them, yes."

"Does that mean we're married?"

He found her lips in the dark. "If you wish it."

"Dominique!" Adrian shouted by the house. "Dominique! Is Madeline here?"

Dominique gave Jeani another deep kiss before

rolling out of the hammock. "Your daughter isn't here, Adrian. Why would she be?"

Adrian held up a lantern stolen off a fishing vessel. "No one's seen her since the noon hours and there's Landers wandering the beaches. One of them split Gregor's lip. The old men say a storm is rolling in off the deep waters. I keep calling for Madeline through the Silence, but she won't answer."

Dominique grabbed a knife he'd left on the tree stump by his hammock. "Jeani, get in the house and lock the door. Don't open it for anyone but me. If the paths flood I may not be back for a day or so, but there's food and water enough. Do you understand?"

She nodded slowly.

He gave her one long, last kiss and ran with Adrian into the jungle after the missing child.

DOMINIQUE'S BORROWED BOOTS SANK SIX INCHES INTO the sucking mud. Jeani would probably insist he shower again before coming to bed, but it would be worth it. He'd found the girl stranded by high tide in a sea cave; he deserved a hero's welcome. There was only one narrow bed in his cabin. He would spend the night warming himself in Jeani's arms. Even just holding her would be bliss.

The cabin was dark. Either the candles had burned down or she'd blown them out, not knowing the custom of keeping a light shining until everyone was home. Wrenching off Adrian's boots, he left them at the door and quietly knocked. "Jeani?"

The unlatched door swung open.

"Jeani?" He lit the oil lamp. The cabin was clean, the blankets neatly folded, the skirt lying on the foot of the bed. Everything was where it should be, except for Jeani. He watched the light of the prison ship slowly sailing past the reefs through the rain and wondered where she might have gone. She said she couldn't magic herself away, and surely no one from Urull would have found her yet.

The lights in the bay bobbed. Within the hour the prison ship would clear the reefs and run full out. To Urull.

CORAL CUT JEANI'S FOOT, BUT SHE PUSHED OFF anyway, swimming closer to the hulking behemoth of a ship. A swell caught her, tugging her out to the planet-wide ocean. Open water, with living things... Panic closed her throat. She gasped, and forced the emotion back. There was no other way.

She flipped on her back so she could float quietly toward the ship, a body lost in the darkness and swells. It wasn't tears on her face, she promised herself, it was just the ocean water. This was the best choice. What would Dominique do if his first-born child was born with fur and fangs?

The villagers would no doubt kill the cub and burn her as a witch. Things like that happened in backwater star systems.

Kicking, she maneuvered as the swells threw her up toward the hull and pulled her back down again. Any sensible ship would have a ladder somewhere. She could only pray to her ancestors that someone had been sensible when designing this one.

The ocean dipped beneath her, a living, sucking, vengeful floor that was out to break her bones. After she got off this planet she was staying station-side for a month. Training in half gravity was no preparation for this. In half gravity she could bounce up the side.

A shadowy figure walked the length of the deck with a lantern held high. The light was yellow and weak, not a danger to her, but she spotted the irregular bump in the rail that marked the ladder.

She waited until the guard passed out of sight and kicked for the ladder. Timing her kicks with the swells, she let the water throw her at the hard metal body of the sailing vessel. It hurt.

Her nails scraped the hull until she finally found purchase halfway down the side. Clinging to the barnacle-encrusted ladder for dear life, she climbed as the waves battered her.

It seemed an eternity before she finally scrambled out of the waves' reach and found herself peering over the dark decks.

Jeani cursed herself for not interrogating the Finn about the ships. She'd let herself get caught up in his touch, in his amusement and wonder as she descrybed the worlds she'd visited, and now she was paying for it. How many people were on a vessel like this? Two? Two hundred? Little details like that mattered right now.

Thunder rolled overhead. Shivering at the thought of lightning striking the metal fixtures of the boat, she hauled herself onto the deck and slid on her belly across to the dubious welcome of a darker shadow.

The smell of death enveloped her. Her eyes adjusted and she peeked under the rough canvas. She was hiding with a pile of shackles encrusted with the blood of the former prisoners.

Lightning split the sky. She listened, ignoring the sound of her heartbeat and her heavy breathing, ignoring the sound of the ocean beating the hull, and found the sounds of people below. Six individual voices, talking, laughing and—she guessed—cursing the weather. None of them spoke in the Standard trade language that Dominique found so easy to use.

Realistically, the population of an entire planet wasn't going to be polyglots, but it would have made her life easier. She didn't even have the equipment needed to record the language and learn it in case she ever came back.

No, Jeani, you're not coming back.

She tried to picture Dominique visiting Nile, or xenophobic Euphrate. The artist's colony still had survivors of the last war with the Finns. They barely tolerated her, endomorphic and an enforcer for Felinium law. Her father would stop talking to her if she brought home a Finn. Not that he talked to her often as it was. Leaving Euphrate had been the final insult. The possibility that she hadn't wanted to see the same view every single day for her entire life was something he couldn't comprehend.

The sound of heavy footsteps heralded the arrival of the lantern holder. Jeani drew her knees to her chest and watched him walk past. The light passed over her bare toes. Jeani closed her eyes and waited. Light fell on her face. The guard said something in the strange language. She ignored him.

A hard boot tapped her shin. "You! What you doing 'ere?"

She opened an eye. "Would you believe I was trying to sleep?"

"Eh? No return trips." He reached down and grabbed her shirt, but couldn't lift her. "Yer a 'eavy one."

She stood up. "I'll take that as a compliment." Grabbing his wrist, she twisted and threw him over her shoulder into the ocean. Dark waves swallowed the lantern's light. One down, five to go.

Hopefully they could all swim. The directorate did not like her filing extensions to her kill list. For some reason, "I'm sorry, sir, but he was in my way and this was the most expedient solution," was not an accepted excuse. She'd probably get a lecture on finding quieter ways to sneak around backwater planets.

If the director was really angry, she'd get another month of basic evasion training.

The ship's course brought them to the edge of a storm, and Jeani watched it cross the decks like a veil.

A weak wind brought the smell of jungle flowers and the bread Dominque had served her.

She inhaled again, trying to catch the scent, but it was nothing. She circled the upper deck twice, but couldn't find a place to hide from the heavy rain.

Reluctantly, she headed below deck. The stench of death and sweaty human flesh was thick here. Terror saturated the wooden passageways. Thick smoke from untrimmed lanterns made her eyes water. The kindest thing she could do for the universe was sink this ship.

Jeani staggered to the end of the passage and found a door swinging open, the latch broken and left unrepaired. The room was empty except for the smell and ghosts of the former prisoners kept here.

Reluctantly, she stepped inside and hid herself at the side of the door. It wasn't the best cover in the world, but with any luck anyone who did a quick search of the room wouldn't notice her. She curled in on herself, thinking of the warmth of Dominique's bed, and the offer in his touch. Shaking, she sat down and leaned against the thrumming hull.

A discordant pulse interrupted the steady rhythm of the engine. It was subtle, like a giant hand knocking on the hull at off intervals, but growing louder. The ship rocked out of time with the rolling waves and Jeani slid across the bare floor.

The giant hand knocked again. Jeani reached for the door, unsure. The crew seemed unconcerned by the arthymic sounds. Perhaps this was normal. She waited tensely for the next knock. Under her feet the deck shivered.

The outer hull bowed... Eased... Broke.

Jeani ducked as broken timber and metal shrapnel flew across the room. Saltwater sprayed her as she screamed. Something wrapped around her leg as she fought to pull herself out the door. She kicked at the obstruction and felt the prick of a hundred tiny knives. Or teeth. She reached into the water, patting at her injured leg—a thick, tough rope was wrapped around her and pulling her backward.

There was a clatter of feet, voices babbling, and three of the crew appeared holding crude harpoons.

The leg being held by the tentacle went numb. Cold seeped up through her veins. Poison.

One of the men grabbed her arm, lifting her away from the creature. His companion drew a short sword and centered it over her knee just above the tentacle.

She jerked her leg sideways, knocking the man away. "What are you doing? Cut the tentacle, not me!"

He screamed and stumbled, sliding on the wet deck.

The cold hit her hip and flooded her abdomen. She took a deep breath, but it was difficult. Breathing took too much energy, too much effort. The cold blood worked its way to her arms. Her fingers trembled.

She flailed as the sea creature tugged her away from the crew. Her abs burned as the forces pulled her apart, and then she let go, falling into the dark water.

Hands grabbed her. The smell of the jungle overwhelmed her even as the cold poison seeped up to her face. She wanted to sleep. Just sleep. Jeani sighed, falling into the lures of Morpheus.

"Jeani. Jeani!"

She opened her eyes and saw Dominique standing over her. Smoky oil lamps rocked back and forth wildly behind him. Her toes still felt wet, but she was lying flat on something. It was an improvement.

"Jeani, what color was the kraken?"

She blinked. "Cold?"

"You feel cold and sleepy?" Dominique asked.

She tried to nod, but it took too much effort.

"Good girl, keep your eyes open a moment longer. There."

Dominique tipped something into her mouth. It smelled foul and tasted like raw sewage. She gagged.

"Millyfish guts. It's the only antidote."

Jeani rolled and spat what she could over the side of the small boat. "It tastes like licking the ground outside an alley on Twylis Three."

"I wouldn't know."

The world bobbed up and down as a pink dawn painted the sky. They were near land, a smog-covered city that smelled worse than the millyfish even at a distance. Her arms began to tingle. Breathing was getting easier. "Why are you here?" she whispered as Dominique rowed the lifeboat with easy confidence.

"Did you think I would let you go?"

"Yes." She tried to shake her head. "I have to go. I need to go back. You can't go with me. Another world. New stars. If you go with me, you can never go back to the islands."

The lifeboat bucked in the tempestuous waves. Dominique cupped her face in his hand. "I never want to come back. I'll go with you, wherever you go."

A coughing fit stole her words. When she could finally draw breath again and the tingling sensation had dropped to her legs, she smiled. "You realize I'm probably headed to my death. Hothi is waiting for me. Those were his ships, and he'll never let me live."

Part of her wanted to wrap her arms around him and babble like a lovesick cub about the worlds she could show him. The more practical part, the part honed through decades as a Felinium enforcer, said that integrating a Finn into Felinium society was asking for trouble. She could handle a fair fight, but she couldn't defend him from the politicking. Eventually he'd realize that this first rush of lust wasn't love. Jeani closed her eyes with a groan.

"What's wrong?" Dominique asked.

"You're going to hate me. If I take you away from all this, you will hate me."

"Do you think it's kinder to tell a man about the wonders of the world, and then snatch it away so he can never touch?"

"Do you realize I don't have a home? I wander, all the time. It's new planets and new languages and new everything every fortnight. I'm about as good at commitment as a fish is at flying!" To emphasize her point a fish leapt out of the water and, instead of dropping at the apogee of its arc like a normal creature, continued to float up and beyond her line of sight. "You have really weird animals on this planet. Most fish don't fly."

"Most couples don't kiss under wedding lights."

Jeani raised an eyebrow. "There's nothing special about spaceships."

Dominique just chuckled.

She closed her eyes and wondered what would happen when she took her new husband home. *Mum,*

Dad... So... I was on this little planet that doesn't even have a name and they've got the funniest tradition. You're going to laugh. You know how some people wish on shooting stars, as if meteorites are luck? Well, there they think seeing a spaceship landing means you're married! Ta-Da! You always wanted me to settle down, didn't you?

Another thought chased that away. "You'll need to get over your nudity issues. Clothes aren't the most popular option where my parents live."

"I'll find a way to adapt."

"Fine. I just want you to understand that you're not allowed to divorce me because my dad likes to walk around naked. My culture doesn't have formal divorces, so there's that too."

Dominique tossed a rope around the pier piling and pulled them to the landing. "I've survived on my own for this long. I think I can adapt to your world."

Grumbling, she sat up and had her first undrugged view of the city of Urull. It was a spaceport, an old, old spaceport with crumbling foundations and the Finn Creation Saga inscribed on a monolith. The control tower was gilded with shiny copper and blue. Someone had turned the baggage trollies into a welded fence. Jeani blinked. "What did you people *do?*"

DOMINIQUE STEPPED ONTO THE PIER, SURREPTITIously putting himself behind Jeani as she swayed in the after effects of the poison. The familiar smell of dead fish, kelp-flour bread, and the stench of thousands of desperate people packed into the small city rolled over him like a bad memory.

"I mean it," Jeani said. "What did your people do to this city?"

"We live in it." Urull looked the same as ever. A city of metal and flotsam hung with rust colored tapestries for doors and curtains. It was dry season, which meant that high tide only flooded the streets once a month. During the rainy season the streets were knee-deep in water and the richer citizens used poling barges to travel. He'd always slogged through the water armed with a chipped knife to defend against sea creatures and gangs.

Jeani walked into the city in awe. "The creation story is wrong."

His heart was racing. There had been nothing new in his world for years, and now there were whole new worlds waiting for him.

She grabbed his hand and dragged him into the streets, heedless of the people staring at her strange clothes and coloring. "Look at this," she ordered, stopping in front of the carved stone that no one had ever managed to destroy.

"It's an eyesore. One of my first memories is some of the older men hacking at it. With the obelisk down they thought they'd have more light for their gardens."

She made a face and lifted her grime-covered boot. "They tried to garden in this?"

"During the dry season."

"No wonder everyone is so sick. This ground has to be saturated with heavy metals. But, here, look at the end of the creation saga." She leaned to the stone and tapped a strangely curved line.

"It's a picture."

She shot him a frown. "You can't read?"

"What's reading?"

Her mouth opened, and then snapped shut. "Reading is a way of communicating with visual signals." She bit her bottom lip then shook her head. "Are you sure you want to leave your home? Everyone I know reads and writes in multiple languages. You're going to be an outcast."

"I'm already an outcast." He caught her hand. "What matters is what you think." The noise of the city was swallowed up in the drumming of his heart. "Do you want me to stay here?"

"No! I mean... I don't know. It's your decision."

He pulled her close so her head rested on his chest. "Let me come with you. I promise, you'll never regret your choice."

Jeani wrapped her arms around his torso. "Let's get through today, and we'll see." She gave him a light kiss on his cheek and turned back to the stone. "The monolith has the standard Finn Creation Saga. Bio-logical warfare on the first planet, soldiers invading a scientific base, the mutation that turns a man into a shark and saves his life after an injury that should have been fatal. The Finn settled this world, which I should have guessed—they like world oceans. Here's the interesting bit: the endomorphs rebelled. The ones who couldn't shift, or who could not survive the mutation injections, attacked the Finns. The flying jellyfish was a defensive precaution, but the Finns still lost."

"Does it matter?" he asked, circling her waist with his arms and pulling her back to him.

"Yeah, unfortunately it does. It means that Hothi can use a settler's claim to back his slave labor here. He's not doing anything wrong if it helps the Finns reclaim this planet."

He stared at the strange carvings for a long moment. "Does this mean you won't go on?"

"No. I'm sure he knows where Ulric is, and this is wrong even if I would have trouble proving it to the Finns. Besides, there's only one way off this planet and Hothi needs to die for me to get to it."

Dominique chuckled. "You're very casual about killing people."

"I never said I was a nice person. I'm better than Hothi, but that doesn't make me good." She shrugged.

Bells clanged along the wide road. Without hesitation, Dominique picked Jeani up, carrying her into an alley before she could protest.

Jeani struggled, pushing away from him with a scowl. "What are you doing?"

"The bells are the warning. The Tyrant's men are scouring the streets for tribute." He noted her confusion and sighed. "The Tyrant gives gifts to the fey, a tribute."

"So, what, a tax? Some guy rings a bell, knocks on your door, and you hand over money and trinkets?"

"No, you lock the door and anyone caught outside is grabbed for tribute." Dominique slid his old knife from the sheath on his thigh. The bells had been the constant terror of his younger years. Twice he'd been caught, dragged into the procession only to cut himself free. He turned the smooth knife handle in his hand, taking comfort from its familiar weight. "If they come for us, we'll fight them off."

Jeani tapped his shoulder. "We're trying to get into the building—"

"Palace."

"Palace." She nodded. "Why not let these nice people escort us in?"

He blinked. A lifetime of avoiding the bells and now she wanted him to waltz in with them as if this were a welcoming procession? The first bell ringer appeared, with guards in red dragging two hapless victims behind him. Both the victims looked like they were in the advanced stages of the Black Blood. Jeani squeezed his arm. "You sure?" Dominique whispered.

"That son of a wolf." Jeani spat, caught up in her own worries. "Shipping sick people off planet instead of quarantining them. That's how plagues spread.

That's why nine hundred died in the colonies of Geffra two years ago. Ulric was hunting down the source." She walked away from him, into the mass of pathetic humans.

Dominique still hesitated. Someone would notice. There was no way they could overlook her strange clothes in the deep black cloth. One guard moved to pull her away, but an icy glare sent him scuttling back. Cursing under his breath, Dominique fell into the throng. At least he looked the part, unshaven, shaggy haired. If he stooped he could pass for an unwanted.

Jeani slowed so she fell back beside him. "What's the routine once everyone gets inside?"

"If I knew that I never would have gone to the islands," he whispered. "Tributes never come back."

"Cheerful. Keep your knife ready. If the layout of the port is anything like other standard Finn designs, we're walking into a maze of circles with Hothi at the center."

"Maybe he won't notice you."

"He'll smell me before we even reach the palace gates. I'm the only Tigya on this planet. Even out of water Hothi would need to cut off his nose before he couldn't smell me coming a mile out."

Dominique took an experimental sniff. Under the layers of Urull Stench, the filth in the streets, and the miasma of illness and despair that clung to the other tributes, he could almost smell something else.

Almost.

The narrow gate swung open with a ground-rattling creak. He grabbed Jeani's hand. "We could still run."

"I'm done running from Hothi," she said grimly. Her expression softened. "If you want to go, I understand. I don't lead an easy life. This is what it's like, every single time: There's a problem, I'm the solution. The odds never get better. Every battle could be my last."

"Then I better come along, to even the odds if nothing else." He squeezed her hand as they went through the ancient gates.

A guard poked him with a truncheon, forcing him to move along or earn a hit. The tributes were led through winding gray corridors with strange smooth walls and weak vines that climbed them only to wither and die. Brown leaves shook as they walked past. Urull was a city of death.

A sudden longing for the life and peace of the islands seized him, closing his throat. Even if the island-born's speech was beyond him, he wanted the life.

As if she understood what he was thinking, Jeani smiled at him. If he wanted her, he had to walk through this place of death. He leaned closer. "You've bewitched me."

She laughed, and it echoed against the alien walls. "Bewitched you? Oh, ancestors, this is a recipe for failure."

He chuckled, because she was laughing and beautiful. "A man can't fall in love the moment he sees a woman?"

"He can fall in lust, but not in love."

He caught her hand. "I fell in love with you the day my sister brought you home. I've searched for you for years. I'll follow you anywhere."

The walls of the tyrant's palace loomed over them. One of the guards prodded Dominique, propelling him through the gate before it swung shut behind them with a clang.

"Last chance to back out," Jeani said as metal scraped against metal and the gate locked behind them.

Dominique drew his knife. "I want to see your fey lights."

JEANI LED THE WAY DOWN THE DUSTY CORRIDORS. THERE was no smell to them. If there were people living in the abandoned control tower, they didn't frequent this area often. A slight breeze brought a corroded smell from up ahead, burning plastic and tar oil. An old ship, falling apart and polluting everything it touched; she knew it as well as she knew the smell of her mother's cooking. Hothi's pollution trails had been a rust-lined path straight to his base.

Ulric had followed them. She had followed them. Still, the reek made her gag.

Dominique frowned at her, but she waved his concern away. "The smell."

He sniffed the air and shrugged. Leaning forward he whispered, "Why did the guards leave?"

"Fear?" she guessed. "How happy would the average citizen of Urull be with coming in here?"

"Not very." He swallowed nervously. "How are we getting out?"

"With luck, we'll fly Hothi's ship out of here. The space museum on Constantinople would love to have it. We shouldn't have any trouble."

At least, without any trouble from her government. There wasn't a way this could end that would improve Finn/Felinium relations.

Six ships sat under a smog-choked sky in the center of the landing arena. Four were obviously slave ships—there was too much damage for anyone to sit at the controls. She wouldn't be leaving on any of those.

Hothi stood under the eaves of his ship by another man, a crippled Sanguis with heavy green tattoos running up his arm. Hothi held a handlight over the tattoos as the other man quivered.

The unholy bastard had given a native Synth tattoos, photosynthetic implants that gave the user a mild buzz from the bacteria's byproduct. A small tat was never enough. Users always added until you saw them wandering naked, wearing nothing but tattoos and a silly grin. They died that way, usually wandering into the deserts in search of more sun and dying of dehydration. Irreversible unless you could find a sunless place like Urull and survive the withdrawals. Curse Hothi to the abyss.

She rapped her knuckles on the wall. "Hello. Did you miss me?"

Hothi turned. "Obviously not. I was worried you wouldn't get here in time."

Jeani gaped at the painfully familiar face, black hair, blue eyes, a trim beard... "Morgan?"

Hothi—no, Morgan—shrugged. "What can I say? I told you sharing information was dangerous."

Her knuckles went white. "Tell me where Ulric is and I'll let you live."

"You'll let me live?" Morgan laughed. "You come to my stronghold and think you can threaten me?"

"Where is Ulric?"

"I sold him to an arms dealer whose clients wanted a beast for space exploration. They'd killed off the native fauna so I sold them a lab rat." He waved his hands in a 'what can you do' gesture. "Ulric was dead within weeks. Take it for what it is. Good news, though, I know a planet that could use a woman of your talents."

Jeani sniffed. "You're cute, Morgan, thinking that you'll get away with this."

"What is there to get away with? You're an endomorph trapped in the body of a Sanguis. No strength. No wit. And you walked in here with my cousin."

Morgan waved hello to Dominique. "He's a Finn, Jeani. And Finn never betray their own."

Jeani looked back at Dominique. "I'm sorry, I forgot to introduce you. Dominique, this is Morgan Finn, your long lost relative and also the man who brought the plague that killed your sister. Morgan, this is Dominique Thierry, my husband as of yesterday."

She didn't wait for Morgan to respond before she barreled toward him. Morgan shuffled back, pushing the drugged Sanguis in her way. She threw the drugged man towards Dominique for what little help he could offer.

"You're a fish out of water, Morgan. Can't shift. Can't swim. Can't bite. And you think you can take a Felinium enforcer in a fight?"

Morgan bumped into the hull of his ship and fumbled for a strange lump of something in his pocket. "Do you know why projectiles are banned in the civilized galaxy?" he asked, raising the bent black object to face level. "My ancestors didn't want humans to have weapons that could level the playing field. They didn't want to fight people who could take advantage of their weaknesses. What they didn't realize was that weapons are a strength, never a weakness."

Rain poured down. Jeani looked up at a smooth gray sky as a chill wind brought fog into the spaceport's landing arena. She heard Dominique behind her, shouting at the Tyrant's guards.

"It had to be done," Morgan shouted over the rain. "Resettlement was the best option for this population. I gave them better lives."

Cold anger settled in Jeani's chest. "You spread disease and killed thousands."

"An oversight. My quarantine controls weren't as strong as they should have been."

"You took a race of people from their natural habitat and relocated them like animals. You did nothing to improve their lives but freely introduced them to diseases and pollutants. How many have you killed out of greed?"

Morgan chuckled. "They're Sanguis, short-lived unwanteds, little better than food. You're a carnivore. You know it's true."

Fog filled the space between them. "I don't eat anything that can talk back." Blue lightning split the sky. The memory of Dominique's scream filled her with panic and dread. The beast had returned. There was a metallic crack and pain in her leg. Jeani dropped to her good knee, staring at the bright red blood running out of her leg.

"Guns," Morgan said conversationally as he walked towards her, fog swirling. "Illegal and unknown in most of the galaxy, but the arms dealer I sold Ulric to was ever so grateful. This was a little token of his admiration. Inferior to what our ancestors had, I suspect. You couldn't fight a war with something that you can't aim." He leaned over her. "I was aiming for your head, by the way."

She pulled herself backward, her leg a burning line of pain. The muscles were trying to knit themselves over the foreign object the … gun … had lodged in her leg. "You found a new world. You could have done anything here. And you chose this?"

Morgan smiled. "What's wrong with being god? I have an entire planet just for me. Is that so terrible?"

A crackling blue tentacle dropped behind Morgan.

"Goodbye, Jeani. I only wish you'd had the sense to stay away."

Ignoring the pain, Jeani leapt, launching herself at Morgan and pushing the Finn back into the electric embrace of the tentacle. He screamed, and latched on to her arm so the current ran through her. Muscles twitched involuntarily; her injured leg twisted. She cried in agony as the world became a black abyss of terrible sensations.

A third voice joined the chorus, and then the pain was over. Shaking, she opened her eyes to see Dominique looking down at her, hurt, worried, abandoned. "I'm sorry."

Strange constellations stretched out below the ship. Dominique ran a hand across his newly shaven chin and watched the growing planet with suspicion. "This is home?"

"This is where I live, Constantinople, capitol of the Felinium and home of the Directorate. That's where my boss works," she added. "I need to tell them what happened to Ulric. His mother and grandmother deserve closure." She shuddered. "He wasn't the best man alive, but no one deserves to die like that."

"And then?"

She shot him a come-hither look over her shoulder. "Then I take some well-deserved vacation time and show you the rest of the galaxy. We'll have to drop by Euphrate so you can meet my family. And then there's this fabulous little colonial planet called Tolza where they have river sex."

"River sex?"

"I don't know what it is either," she said, shrugging, "but it sounds like fun."

Dominique chuckled and pulled her into his lap. She had promised new things every fortnight, and he intended to enjoy everything his fey lady offered.

Dear Reader,

Thank you for spending some time in my fictional world. I hope you enjoyed reading about Jeani and Dominique as much as I did writing about them. I admit, I wouldn't mind spending some time relaxing on the beaches with the island-born; I have a fondness for tropical paradises. And while I don't spend as much time at the beach as I would like, you can usually find me on Twitter as @LianaBrooks. I'm also on FaceBook as Liana Brooks. Feel free to come say hello any time!

~ Liana

ABOUT THE AUTHOR

Liana Brooks was born in San Diego, California. Years later she was disappointed to learn that The Shire was not some place she could move to, nor was Rider of Rohan an acceptable career choice. Studying marine biology so she could play with sharks seemed to be the only alternative. After college Liana settled down to work as a full-time author and mother because logical career progression is something that happens to other people. When she grows up, Liana wants to be an Evil Overlord and take over the world.

In the meantime, she writes sci-fi and SFR in between trips to the beach. She can be found wearing colorful socks on the Emerald Coast, or online at www.lianabrooks.com.

CHAPTER ONE

I knew from the first time I saw my wife that I wanted her naked. Of course, seven minutes later I wanted revenge. It wasn't that she had handed me my first defeat or ruined my chances for world domination that year, it was the way she kissed me good-bye. She sent my head spinning, then walked away as if I were the least important person in the world.

Once my arm healed, I stole some new equipment, cloned some new minions, and I felt a little different.

I wanted revenge, with a side order of naked.

ACROSS THE DINNER table, Tabitha devoured him with dark, ocean-blue eyes. She put a bite of lettuce in her mouth, full lips pursing around it. Eating salad never looked so good. Her tongue darted out to lick away a stray drop of dressing. She winked at him, promising with every move to do the same to him. "It's almost bedtime," she said, her voice husky and luscious.

"I don't wanna go to bed!" one of the quads screamed.

"What about cake? Don't we get birthday cake?" another asked.

Evan winked back at his wife from the far side of the table, separated by a few feet and four precocious just-turned-five-year olds, all as stunning as their mother with big, round eyes and hair that fell in loose curls meant to trap hairbrushes and sticky substances. He had to peek at the eyes to see who was talking. Maria had green eyes, Angela's eyes were blue like Tabitha's, Delilah's eyes were brown like his, and Blessing—their stillborn who miraculously survived—had purple eyes. The waif in question had blue eyes.

"Angela," Evan said, "after dinner it's pajama time, and then story time."

"Mommy doesn't have a bedtime!" Angela wailed.

Tabitha winked at him again. "Tell you what, tonight Mommy will go to bed the same time you do. Right after we eat cake." She leaned over to give Angela a hug.

All Evan could see was the deep V plunge of her tight blue shirt. Oh, yeah. Crime didn't always pay, but altering someone's moral compass sure put the O's back in the bedroom.

The cake was split into fourths, equal parts purple, white, green, and blue so each girl could have her favorite color in the cake. Baking four cakes was unreasonable; there weren't any grandparents left to celebrate with, and neighbors had an annoying habit of asking uncomfortable questions.

Saying little things like, "You look just like Doctor Charm! Do you remember him? Whatever happened to that guy? Do you know how hard it is to put together a good Villains vs. Heroes fantasy league without him?" made for awkward evenings.

So they had a quiet family party. Cake, then presents, after which he hurried the girls off to bed so he could read Dilly Duck's ABCs in record time before rushing to the bedroom, hoping to catch Tabitha still in the shower.

She was already out and wearing a blue satin robe that caressed her skin in exactly the way he wanted to. Rose-scented candles cast sensuous shadows on the walls.

Tabitha turned, lips curved in an inviting smile. Long fingers twined with the sash of her robe. She tossed her honey-blonde hair in the way she always did when she was about to argue, posing with feet apart and one hand casually resting on her waist. "Sweetie, we need to talk."

Evan wiped grease-stained hands on his jeans as he forced a smile. "Sure, babes, anything you want."

"Really?" She slunk forward, all sinewy limbs and doe eyes. "Promise?" Tabitha nuzzled his nose. One hand flirted up the back of his neck to play with his hair. The other traveled downward, right to his zipper.

Oh, yes, the little Morality Machine in the basement was working just fine. Another thirty, maybe forty years of this and he'd consider retiring. Or turning the machine down so his wife wasn't quite a sex kitten every day of the week. Maybe only days with Y in them.

"Sweetie?" She nibbled his ear. "I want to go back to work."

"What?" Evan actually pushed himself away from her, something he wasn't sure was possible in any other circumstance.

Tabitha tucked her chin and pouted.

"Tabby-cat, I love you, but work? I've got my... stuff... in the lab. I'm busy. And we can't afford daycare for the girls. We're barely making ends meet as it is. Do you really want to go back to being Zephyr Girl? Crime fighting is a game for the young, baby. You're not nineteen anymore."

"I'm twenty-nine. A very"—her hips pressed against his tight jeans just so—"very healthy twenty-nine."

He shivered at her touch. "You're cheating."

"I want to do this, Evan." She ground against the thick denim.

"You can do me all you want, baby."

She stepped back, frowning. "I'm serious."

"So am I." Evan sighed, reaching for his wife. "Sweetie, I love you, but what's the point in being a superhero? The government stipend barely covers the dry-cleaning bill. If it's money you want, write another tell-all superhero book. The Spanish Mask sold his third last month."

Tabitha crossed her arms. "I don't want to write another book just for royalties while you're between jobs."

He waved a finger at her. "I'm not between jobs. I work freelance in the computer business. I'm self-employed. That's not the same as being between jobs."

"Between paychecks then."

"We will have a solid income. This project I'm working on, Tabby-cat, it's going to set us up for life. We're never going to worry about money again. I promise. Give me a couple of weeks and everything is going to be perfect." He caught her hand and pulled her into his arms. The faint scent of her spicy perfume left him dizzy with need.

She rested her head on his chest. "I want to save the world. Have you seen the news, Evan? An entire town in Kansas held hostage for a week by a bomb scare before a superhero was able to get in to defuse the situation. A week! I could have that done between grocery shopping and paying the bills. Ten minutes, no pulling punches."

"I know, baby. No one is better at this stuff than you. But I need you at home, Tabby. Having you out there scares me. I'm terrified I'd lose you. Why don't you wait until I finish this project? I'll be done by the time the election rolls around. Two more weeks. Once I get paid we'll look at this again. I have that armor design for you, I just need some time to put it together."

Tabitha sighed. "You've been saying that since we got married."

"Well, my nights are busy." He nibbled her ear as he tugged her sash loose. "Are you complaining?"

Tabitha stretched against him, sending a delightful frisson of lust up his spine. "I thought you gave up the super villain schemes."

He twitched. "I did, baby. Of course I did."

"But you're keeping me here. Isn't that a little selfish? Just a teeny-tiny bit super villain-ish?" She slipped her hand between his pants and his skin.

"Ah!" He caught her hand so he could think clearly. "Not selfish. Necessary. Like oxygen or sex."

"Don't you mean water?"

"No, definitely sex." Evan slid her robe off and tossed it into a corner. "Come here, Tabby-cat, I'll make you purr."

She tugged at his shirt, pulling it up. The shirt joined the robe on the other side of the room. "What are you doing down in that lab?" she asked as her hands drew lazy circles on his back.

Ten seconds, that's all he'd need to get her panties off. Three more to drop his pants. "What was the question?"

"What are you doing in the lab? What's this project?"

"Oh, computer stuff. I told you. To help tally everything on election night. I'm trying to make the process run smoother so we don't have to worry about recounts."

"Hmmm." She gave him a dubious frown.

Tabitha was built like a supermodel and had a superhero name straight from Campy Comics, but her brain was Mensa all the way. "And this computer program has nothing to do with world domination, or get-rich-quick schemes?"

Evan contrived to look wounded. "Tabby-cat, how can you ask that?"

"Because you spent ten years as a villainous criminal mastermind?"

"I wasn't a mastermind, I was a super villain, there's a difference. Masterminds are just thugs with money. My crimes had artistic flare. I was practically Robin Hood! Robbing from the rich and scandalous, and giving to me."

"Robin Hood gave to the poor," Tabitha said with a laugh. "You were never poor."

He caught her hand, pulling her close. "Poor is relative. Besides, I'm reformed now. You showed me the error of my wicked ways. Although"—he leaned in for a kiss—"if you'd like to remind me why I gave up a lucrative life of crime, I have the evening free."

EVEN VILLAINS GO TO THE MOVIES
Heroes & Villains Book #2

When your mother is America's Superhero Sweetheart and your daddy's the Number One Super Villain, you grow up feeling a little conflicted.

Available from all major online retailers.

www.InkprintPress.com

EVEN VILLAINS HAVE INTERNS
Heroes & Villains Book #3

It's Chicago's favorite city son vs Delilah, daughter of Dr. Charm. America's second city will never know what hit it.

Available from all major online retailers.

www.InkprintPress.com